DATE DUE			DEC 0 5

THE HOTEL CAT

THE
HOTEL
CAT

Story and Pictures by
Esther Averill

THE NEW YORK REVIEW
CHILDREN'S COLLECTION
New York

THIS IS A NEW YORK REVIEW BOOK
PUBLISHED BY THE NEW YORK REVIEW OF BOOKS
1755 Broadway, New York, NY 10019
www.nyrb.com

Library of Congress Cataloging-in-Publication Data
Averill, Esther Holden.
The hotel cat / by Esther Averill.
p. cm.— (New York Review children's collection)
Summary: Relates the rise of Tom, the hotel cat, from catcher of mice in
the cellar to successful upstairs cat in charge of the hotel's guest cats.
ISBN 1-59017-159-4 (alk. paper)
[1. Cats—Fiction. 2. Hotels, motels, etc.—Fiction.] I. Title. II. Series.
PZ7.A935Ho 2005
[Fic]—dc22
2005004469

ISBN-13: 978-1-59017-159-2
ISBN-10: 1-59017-159-4

Cover design by Louise Fili Ltd

Printed in the United States of America on acid-free paper
1 3 5 7 9 10 8 6 4 2

For Ursula Nordstrom,
our friend and sponsor,
from the loving Cat Club

Contents

In the Cellar
of the Royal

The Royal Hotel stood eight stories high, but the towering skyscrapers that had sprung up all around it made it look like what it was: the oldest hotel in New York City.

People in the street, as they passed by, would often exclaim, "My! Is the old Royal still standing?" But the Royal, of course, was still standing, and it was still carrying on its business of supplying room and bed to persons in need of shelter.

1

When the cat first saw the Royal, he was young and hungry, and he had no home. All night he'd been roaming the streets in search of food, and he hadn't found one bite to eat. Now that morning had come, he wondered which way to turn.

The skyscrapers surrounding the Royal Hotel did not attract this cat. In bright new buildings such as these, he'd never had much luck. The shabby Royal seemed more friendly, and when he drew close to it, he liked it even better. Its old bricks had a pleasant, crumby smell.

The young cat waited until nobody was looking. Then he slipped through a side door that was partly open and climbed down into the cellar. Mr. Fred, the Furnace Man, took pity on him and gave him some breakfast.

The young cat purred his thanks, gobbled the food, and thought to himself, "Maybe I can make myself useful. Maybe I can earn a supper."

Luck again favored the young cat. The old Hotel Cat, who had worked down here for many years, had recently retired and gone to live in the country. Rats and mice were scampering across the cellar floor. The young cat immediately began to chase away the creatures. He worked so hard that in the evening Mr. Fred gave him more than supper. Mr. Fred gave him the job of Hotel Cat in the cellar of the Royal.

With the job, the new Hotel Cat received a room of his own near the boiler of the furnace. And in Mr. Fred he found a kind-hearted friend who provided him with two meals (breakfast and supper) every day. And finally—oh, joy of joys to this young cat who'd never had a name—Mr. Fred called him Tom.

Easy was the life that seemed to lie ahead of Tom down in the cellar of the Royal Hotel. His work with the rats and mice required only his daytime care. But nights were his own—and he was young.

Tom's Lady,
Mrs. Wilkins

At night, the young Hotel Cat would lie awake on his bed in the cellar and wonder what it was like on the floors over his head. Mr. Fred, with a wave of an arm, had called the whole building the Royal Hotel. But Tom, owing to the gap between cat talk and human talk, had not been able to ask questions about the business of the Royal. All he knew of any hotel life was this cellar, where he worked at chasing rats and mice. He was eager to explore the world above him.

One evening after supper, Tom washed his grey coat and white shirt front with extra care. After that, he waited until Mr. Fred had gone to sleep, and it seemed time indeed for most people to have taken themselves to bed. Then Tom climbed the cellar stairs, pushed open the cellar door, which was never really closed, and found himself near the middle of the first, or ground, floor of the Hotel.

There were more lights here than he had expected, and a number of people were sitting in a waiting room. Now and then a person carrying a suitcase walked in from the street.

"Maybe the next floor will be quieter," thought Tom hopefully, for he did not enjoy meeting people. Few human beings had been kind to him. Mr. Fred was the great exception, but Tom felt sure there would never be another Mr. Fred.

Tom now scurried back to a dark end of the building and discovered some wonder-

ful broad stairs that went up and around
through a stairwell as far as his eye could
reach. The dimness of light in this stairwell
and the dust on the stairs told him that people seldom came here, and he began slowly
to climb these stairs. They delighted him

with their musty smells of happenings from long ago.

When Tom reached the landing on the second floor, he discovered, on his left, a double door that stood partly open. He stepped to the doorway and looked into a long, tall, shadowy room, lit only by glowings which filtered through the windows from street lamps. The room seemed very empty, but like the stairway, it held memories. The memories here were like the ghosts of pleasant, old-time people moving gracefully across the dusty floor.

Suddenly, from behind Tom, came the real, true rustle of a skirt. He turned and saw a small bent woman coming down the hall. She walked slowly toward him. It was her dark, full, shining skirt that trailed along the floor and made the rustle.

"My dear, don't be afraid. Don't run away," she called to him.

Her voice was the gentlest he had ever heard, and he was not afraid. He stayed

right in the doorway and let her come to him.

"My dear, who may you be?" she asked.

"Tom, the Hotel Cat," he replied. And since he was an honest cat, he added, "I do the cellar work. This is my first trip upstairs."

"Tom," said she, "I am Mrs. Wilkins. My room is in a passage down the hall. I like to walk while others sleep. I love these halls. I have lived among them for a long, long time."

"Ma'am, what was our Hotel like in other days?" asked Tom, thinking it would be good for a Hotel Cat to know something about the history of his place.

"My dear," said she, "maybe the paint was brighter. But I like the Royal this way, too."

"Ma'am, what's this big room here?"

"Ah, Tom, it's the old grand ballroom of the Royal. I can remember the nights when this ballroom blazed with lights, and people danced, and those who didn't dance might

10

sit on gold chairs lined up against the walls. The gold chairs—alas!—are gone. Everything is gone except the grand piano over in the corner."

Tom was surprised that he could understand each word spoken by Mrs. Wilkins. She, for her part, seemed to miss nothing of what Tom wished to say. This, of course, was not the case between Tom and Mr. Fred. Conversation in the cellar had to be about simple things, such as rats and mice, breakfast and supper, the weather and the boiler.

"Ma'am, would you tell me more about the Royal and what it's like today?" said Tom.

"Yes, Tom, let us go and sit on the landing of the grand stairway. We can talk there comfortably because nobody will disturb us. Nobody ever comes to this old part of the building except Mr. Peter, the night watchman, and he has just gone by."

Tom and Mrs. Wilkins walked to the

landing of the grand stairway, which was the broad stairway that he had just climbed. Mrs. Wilkins seated herself on the edge of the landing, rested her feet on the stair below, and spread her shining skirt around her ankles. Tom sat close beside her and listened carefully while she told him that a few of the Hotel guests were old people who, like herself, had come here many years ago and remained. Most guests, however, were traveling people who arrived with a suitcase and stayed only for a night or two before continuing their journeys.

"I saw travelers down on the first floor, and then they came upstairs," said Tom.

"The first floor," explained Mrs. Wilkins, "is the business floor. The rooms where the guests stay begin here on the second floor and continue upward, from floor to floor, through all eight floors of our Hotel. Some night, my dear, you must take a look at those old floors. They are filled with interesting halls and passages."

Halls and passages! Those words stirred Tom's imagination. He thought to himself what fun it would be if he could find night work to do up here. But the question was, Had other cats already claimed the territory?

So he said in a cautious voice, "I suppose the Hotel keeps others like me to do the upstairs work."

"No, Tom, you are the one and only Hotel Cat of the Royal."

This news delighted him, and he cried, "I'll come up at night and chase away your rats and mice."

"My dear, we have no rats or mice up

here," said Mrs. Wilkins gently.

"No rats, no mice, and I was hoping to find a little work to do up here at night," sighed Tom.

"But, Tom, you are young, and if you search hard enough, you will find night work to do upstairs."

Tom brightened at those words.

And Mrs. Wilkins went on to say, "Meanwhile, there is something you might do for me."

Tom cocked his ears.

"My dear," said she, "you might keep an old lady company for a little while, just now and then, whenever you have time."

"My Lady," he cried, "I'll come up every night. Tell me where we shall meet and when."

She replied, "This is a good spot. And midnight, which is the hour when we first met, is a good time. Our night watchman, Mr. Peter, will let you know when midnight comes."

"Does he speak cat talk?" asked Tom.

"Not a word of it, but Mr. Peter patrols our halls faithfully, and you will find him on the different floors at hours that never change. You will soon learn which hour is midnight."

"My Lady, shall we meet again tomorrow night?" asked Tom wistfully.

"Tomorrow night," said she, pulling her many scarves around her shoulders. "My dear, it's time for me to go. Have I forgotten anything? I can be forgetful."

Tom stood up, glanced about, and saw a bag lying at the other side of her.

"Your bag," he said.

"My handbag with my room key in it," murmured Mrs. Wilkins. She gathered up her handbag, rose to her feet, and said, "And now would our Hotel Cat be kind enough to take me safe to my room?"

Tom of the Royal escorted his Lady down the hall. She walked slowly because of her trailing skirt, and he, who walked beside

her, was careful not to tangle in it. Soon they went into a little passage, where his Lady lived. As the door of her room was closed, he stood with her while she fumbled for her key and unlocked the door. He did not move while she entered her room, waved good night, and closed the door.

"My Lady, don't forget to lock your door," he called.

He waited until he heard the key turn in the lock. Then, as it was growing late, the one and only Hotel Cat of the Royal returned to his office in the cellar. He felt that his first exploration of the world above had been a great success. He had climbed one flight of the old grand stairway, seen the deserted ballroom, and made a precious human friend—his Lady, Mrs. Wilkins. Her words of hope were ringing in his ears: "Tom, if you search hard enough, you will find night work to do upstairs."

Trouble Upstairs

Mrs. Wilkins may have been forgetful, but she never forgot her midnight meetings with the young Hotel Cat. Indeed, she came to them early, and Tom would find her waiting among the shadows on the second-floor landing of the old grand stairway, close to the deserted ballroom.

His Lady would be sitting there with her full skirt spread round her ankles and holding a little paper-napkin package of midnight snacks for him to munch. Not only did he enjoy the tidbits, he loved her company. Sometimes she would tell him about the old days at the Royal. More often she would hum tunes from those bygone times. Then he would escort his Lady to the door of her room and remain there until he heard her key turn in the lock.

After the midnight meetings, and before them, Tom explored the upstairs floors in search of work. Each floor contained a long, lofty hall, crisscrossed by passages that ran every which way. Halls and passages were lined with wooden doors that usually remained closed. Behind the doors were the rooms of the Hotel guests.

Occasionally a guest—some traveler with a suitcase—stepped from the elevator and opened a door. But the door would be closed quickly, and the guest might be heard taking off his shoes and going to bed. The later it grew, the quieter grew the Hotel and the more Tom loved to roam through the halls.

"All this is my territory," he told himself. "All these floors are mine to manage. How, oh, how? There are indeed no rats or mice up here, and the human guests who come and go are not my business. But Mrs. Wilkins said that if I searched hard enough, I'd find work to do. I'll keep quietly looking. When I've found something, I'll surprise my Lady with the news."

 One night, as he prowled through a hall, his nose caught the smell of a strange cat. "A cat has dared enter my territory," muttered Tom.

The blood of the Hotel Cat boiled, and he wanted to drive the invader from the territory. So he traced the invader's smell to the closed door of a room. Inside the room, though a man was asleep and snoring, the cat was awake and stirring. But the door stood in the way of a fight and reminded Tom that the cat was a guest of the Hotel.

"What a guest!" thought Tom. "He's probably a spoiled pet accompanying his master on a pleasant little journey. Pet cat! Bah!"

Tom hated all that he had ever seen of pet cats. Back in the days when he was a hungry kitten living on the streets, he had climbed fire escapes and looked through windows. And often he had watched those darlings turn up their noses at platters of fine food and go off and scratch some furniture. Pet cats, he believed, did nothing but behave badly.

"But not at my Hotel," he now decided. "At my Hotel, they shall behave. Oh, ho! Here's my chance. Here's the work I've wanted. Cat guests shall be my business."

Tom stepped right up to the door of the cat guest whom he had just discovered and in a stern voice called, "I am Tom, the Hotel Cat. Stay in your room and don't scratch the Hotel furniture."

The cat guest answered Tom with a hiss. But Tom didn't care. He walked away, believing he had done what a Hotel Cat ought to do—protect his Hotel from harm. Yet somehow he didn't feel like telling his Lady, Mrs. Wilkins, what had happened.

The next night Tom found that the cat guest had left the Royal. However, a few nights later a new cat guest turned up in another room, and Tom gave him the same speech: "I am Tom, the Hotel Cat. Stay in your room and don't scratch the Hotel furniture."

The cat guest answered Tom with a hiss. But Tom didn't care. He walked away, believing he had again done the right thing. Yet again he didn't feel like telling his Lady about the night work he was doing.

By the following night, the second cat guest had also departed. But after a few more nights, Tom located a third cat guest, to whom he delivered the same words of advice: "Stay in your room and don't scratch the Hotel furniture."

This guest—alas!—answered Tom with a terrible growl, and jumped down from somewhere and upset something with an awful crash. Then he rushed to his side of the door and shrieked, "Mind your own business!"

The remark cut Tom to the very bones and made him feel he was failing in his night work. Even worse had been the crash. The night watchman, Mr. Peter, had heard it and was coming. Tom scurried away and hid in the dark ballroom until midnight. By then he was ready to tell his Lady everything.

He found Mrs. Wilkins sitting, as usual, on the landing of the old grand stairway, near the ballroom. After they had said Good Evening, he ate his tidbits (scraps of salmon) in silence. Then suddenly he exclaimed, "Guess what?"

His Lady shook her head. "Tell me, my dear."

Tom, like many other young cats who have a difficult story to relate, found it easiest to begin at the end. "Just now I was told to mind my own business," he said.

"Who told you that?" she asked.

"That goon."

"What goon?"

"That cat upstairs."

"Whereabout upstairs?" asked Mrs. Wilkins.

"He was in a guest room on the fifth floor. He'd moved in there with his owner."

"What kind of cat was this cat guest?" continued Mrs. Wilkins.

"A pet cat. That's all I know. His door was closed," replied Tom.

"My dear, what made him speak to you like that?"

"Nothing. All I did was to tell him "Stay in your room and don't scratch the Hotel furniture."

"Ah!" said Mrs. Wilkins thoughtfully.

"And then guess what, my Lady?"

Mrs. Wilkins shook her head.

"That creature growled at me," said Tom, "and jumped down from somewhere, and knocked something over with an awful crash, and told me to mind my own business."

"And what, my dear, did you reply to that?"

"My fur bristled, but I held my tongue because Mr. Peter heard the crash and was coming, and I scrammed. I thought I'd keep away from Mr. Peter until I'd spoken with you about my night work. You see, my Lady, I thought I'd found something to do. I thought I'd make cat guests my business. What do you think of that?"

"I think, Tom, you have found your true night work. Cat guests should be the business of a Hotel Cat."

"Well then, my Lady, what's wrong with what I tell our guests? Isn't it the business of a Hotel Cat to protect his place from damage?"

"Yes, Tom, but there is another part of hotel work that is nearly as important."

"What?" he demanded.

She stroked his cheek and answered, "Every hotel worker ought to make the stay of a guest as pleasant as possible."

"My Lady," Tom objected, "our cat guests are here one night and gone the next."

She said, "But while our guests are here,
their happiness does matter."

"Happiness!" he cried. "Why, those guests
of ours are play cats. Let them amuse themselves."

"Tom, keep an open mind about our

guests," urged Mrs. Wilkins. "It takes all kinds of cats to make a world, and sooner or later they will turn up at the Royal. No matter who they are, remember they are away from home and may be homesick. Perhaps they don't even know the next stop on their journey. So it's the duty of the Hotel Cat to give them a real, warm welcome, as if he wished their stay with us to be a happy one."

"And if I do all that?" demanded Tom.

"Why then, my dear, you are on your way to becoming a truly fine Hotel Cat."

"It's what I'd like to be," sighed Tom.

Thus, by the following night, Tom of the Royal had thought up a friendly Welcome Speech. But when he toured the floors, he found that the mind-your-own-business guest of the night before had moved away, and no new cats seemed to have arrived.

Until now, Tom had not used any steady method for touring the floors. He decided the time had come for him to give them a regular night patrol, which would keep him in touch with everything that was happening. So each night he started his patrol on the second floor, where the guest rooms began, and ended it on the eighth, or top, floor.

The territory, of course, was too large for a cat to cover inch by inch. What Tom did was this: He stopped at the important points on a floor and cast sharp looks, cocked his ears, sniffed the air, and twitched his whiskers. His whiskers had a radar power that brought him messages of what his eyes, ears, and nose could not detect. But night after night went by, and none of his powers revealed the arrival of any new cat guests.

Mrs. Wilkins tried to comfort him by saying, "My dear, that's the way with hotel work. Business may be dull one night and brisk the next."

But Tom felt deeply worried. He feared the news had got about that Tom of the Royal was doing a poor job. He feared he had lost his chance of becoming a fine Hotel Cat—one who knew how to make his cat guests happy with a few pleasant words of welcome.

The Cats in Room 811

At last, one night—it was during the winter that went down in New York City history as the Winter of the Big Freeze—the Hotel Cat detected some business. He was on the top floor of the Royal, making the final round of his patrol, when his whiskers twitched, and he tiptoed to the closed door of Room 811.

Not one cat, but more than one had moved into this room. Right now they were sniffing at the crack between the door and the floor. What a lot of sniffing! What a lot of noses! So many cats could do real damage to the Hotel. But Tom kept an open mind, and in his most courteous voice he said, "Good evening."

The sniffing stopped.

"Good evening, sir," replied the gentle, steady voice of a young he-cat who sounded about Tom's age.

"I am Tom, the Hotel Cat," continued Tom. "Welcome to the Royal. I hope you will enjoy your stay with us."

"Thank you, Tom," replied the same gentle voice on the other side of the door.

Then Tom said, "Make this Hotel your home away from home. However, in the interests of your own safety, I must beg you not to leave your room. And oh, please don't scratch the Hotel furniture."

"Our master brought our scratching post with us," said the gentle voice.

Tom was about to bid good night to 811, but curiosity got the best of him. He asked,

"Do you always travel with a scratching post?"

"We aren't really traveling," replied the voice. "We're New York City cats. Our boiler at home burst. We've come to live at your hotel until we can get back our heat. We've brought enough things with us for quite a stay."

"How many of you have come?" asked Tom.

"Our master, Captain Tinker, and his three cats," the voice explained. "I'm the oldest cat. I am Edward. Then there's my younger brother, Checkers, and our little sister, Jenny."

This was the longest conversation Tom had ever held with a cat guest. It had been agreeable, but Tom could think of nothing more to say. Besides, the hour was growing late, and he did not wish to keep his Lady, Mrs. Wilkins, waiting.

"Edward," he said, "I hope you and Checkers and Jenny will be very happy at the Royal. And now, since I have other business to attend to, I must say good night."

Tom was moving away from the door of 811 when another voice—a bright one from within the room—called out, "Hi, Tom! I'm Checkers. You haven't said one word to me."

"Checkers, welcome to the Royal Hotel," replied Tom.

Tom continued on his way. But that bright voice overtook him. "Tom, how's the boiler at the Royal?"

"New, brand new," Tom called back proudly.

"I bet," cried the voice, "I bet it's the only new thing in this old hotel."

Old Hotel! Why, that was none of the Bright One's business. Tom dashed angrily to the door and shouted, "Old Hotel! Take back those words."

"Tom, forgive me," replied Checkers in a voice that had turned as smooth as butter. "I meant 'old and very interesting.' "

"That's more like it," observed Tom.

"Our noses told us so," continued Checkers. "We've spent hours sniffing at the crack between our door and the floor. Your halls out there are filled with smells of other days —nice, interesting old smells."

"The Royal is indeed a nice, interesting old place," said Tom, whose anger had died away.

"How big?" asked Checkers.

"Eight floors, three hundred rooms," replied Tom.

"Which room are we in?" continued Checkers.

"Room 811, on the eighth, or top, floor. And be sure you stay in 811," said Tom.

"Why can't we step out and see what your hotel is like?" asked Checkers.

"There are miles and miles of halls, and you'd get lost and maybe not get found," said Tom. "And now, Master Checkers, I really have to go."

But a small voice came through the door: "Tom! It's me! It's Jenny."

The voice, though small and shy, was so warm and friendly that it held Tom to the spot.

"Jenny, what is it?" he inquired.

"My brothers forgot to tell you that we think 811 is a very pretty room," she said.

"Thank you," said Tom, whose heart was touched by those kind words of praise for his Hotel.

"And we've had fun talking with you," continued Jenny.

"Thank you," said Tom, and he felt a glow spread through him.

"Tom, will you call on us again?" she asked.

Tom usually called only once at the door of new arrivals. But, of course, he had never been invited to return. Besides, how could he say No to such a friendly little cat as Jenny?

"I'll call again," he promised.

"Exactly when?" she asked.

"Night's my time for patrolling these halls," he answered.

"Will you come tomorrow night?" she asked.

"Yes, Jenny, tomorrow night, around this

hour. But I may have time only for a word or two."

"Tom, to us cooped up inside this room a word or two would mean a lot. Oh, thank you, Tom!" cried Jenny.

Tom dashed along the hall to the other end of the building and hurried down the old grand stairway. He found Mrs. Wilkins waiting for him, as usual, among the shadows on the second-floor landing.

"My Lady," he began, "I'm sorry to be late. Three new cats in 811. I used my friendly Welcome Speech. It worked. But are they talkers!"

"Ah!" said Mrs. Wilkins in an interested voice as she opened his paper-napkin package.

Tom gobbled the tidbits (roast chicken), wiped his mouth and whiskers, and continued, "Those three cats are New York City cats. Boiler burst at home. They've brought along their scratching post, and they plan to stay here quite a while. They asked me to

38

call on them again tomorrow night. I said I would, but now I wish I'd said I wouldn't."

"My dear, you really ought to call on them tomorrow night," said Mrs. Wilkins.

"Why?" demanded Tom.

"Because," said she, "a Hotel Cat ought to keep up a friendly relation with his guests. He should continue to call on them for as long as they are here so as to make their whole visit a happy one."

"My Lady," wailed Tom, "what shall I say tomorrow night to those guests in 811? I've already told them about the number of rooms and floors we have, and about our new boiler."

"My dear, I am sure you will find something else to say. It doesn't have to be much —just a little something interesting for your guests to think about."

Mrs. Wilkins rose, and Tom, as was his custom, took her safe to her room. Then he climbed down to his own cozy room, which was near the new boiler, jumped up on his bed, and lay down to think.

"Where in the world," he wondered, "can I find anything interesting to say to the cats in 811? I'll not tell them that the Royal has a Lady who speaks perfect cat talk. I'll keep Mrs. Wilkins to myself."

He tucked his chin between his paws to think more clearly, and he thought, "But I can tell them some of the things my Lady has told me. I'll tell those cats about the history of this famous old Hotel. A short History Speech—oh, ho!—should interest them and help Tom of the Royal keep up a friendly relation with his guests."

The Runaway Guest

In Tom's life, a friendly relation with other cats was something quite new. Out on the streets, where he had spent his early life, he'd had to scrabble to find food, and there had been no time for making friends with any cat. So, on the day following the arrival of the cats in 811, Tom worked very hard on a little History Speech aimed at interesting those three guests and helping him keep up a friendly relation with them.

He would say to them "The Royal Hotel, where you are staying, is the oldest hotel in New York City. None was more elegant. People like princesses and grand dukes used to live here, and at night our ballroom blazed with lights. Times may have changed, but the glamor of the old days lingers in our halls and walls."

Night came, and as he climbed the cellar stairs, Tom repeated the Speech to himself. He felt proud of it and could hardly wait to deliver it at the door of 811, which, because of its high location, would be the last stop of his patrol.

As he made his rounds, he found no new cat guests to delay him. Everything seemed calm, except for once when his radar whiskers twitched and told him of a little scurry somewhere among the floors below him.

"A mouse up here!" thought Tom with surprise. "Oh, well, the mouse can wait. I'll go straight ahead and deliver my Speech."

But on the top floor, as he moved along

the hall toward 811, there suddenly rose, from the floor, the scent of a cat. Tom could see that the door of 811 was closed. This scent, however, belonged to one of those cats. Tom rushed to their door and demanded, "Which of you escaped?"

"Edward!" came the mournful answer from two cats next to their side of the door.

"Edward, the oldest of you all!" exclaimed Tom. "I am surprised at Edward. Last night he sounded like a steady, reliable cat."

"He is!" cried Checkers. "But his nose got the best of him."

"What has his nose got to do with breaking a Hotel Rule?" asked Tom impatiently.

"Edward has the nose of a poet," explained little Jenny. "All day long he sniffed

EDWARD HAS THE NOSE OF A POET

at this crack between our door and the floor. He said his nose caught the smells of wonderful old happenings out there in your lofty halls. He said he'd write a poem about your hotel if he could go out and sniff some more and see things with his own eyes."

"I could have told him the history of the place," muttered Tom, who regretted that his History Speech had gone up in smoke. "But this," he told himself, "is not the time to feel sorry for myself. This is the time to rescue a runaway guest."

Jenny was pleading with him. "Oh, don't be angry with Edward."

"I'm not angry. I'm worried," said Tom.

"Will you help us find him?" asked Jenny.

"I'll do my best," said Tom. "Now tell me quickly what happened."

Jenny and Checkers together related the story. It had happened at suppertime. Their master, Captain Tinker, had gone out to buy his three cats something to eat. When he returned with his bundle and opened their door, Edward slipped quietly past the Captain's feet. The Captain called for Edward to come back. But Edward, who had always been so good and so obedient, did not come.

The Captain immediately laid his bundle inside the room and started off to search for Edward. The Captain had been careful to shut the door so that Checkers and Jenny could not search, too. A long time passed before the Captain returned. He had not found Edward.

The Captain fed Checkers and Jenny and left the room again to hunt for Edward. The Captain was out there looking for him now, and it was a pity because the Captain's legs were acting up from rheumatism brought on by the broken boiler at home.

"I'm sorry for your master," interrupted Tom. "He might search this Hotel from top to bottom and maybe never find Edward. The place is so big that your master could go one way and your brother go another, and their two ways never meet."

"Tom,"—it was Checkers who was speaking—"couldn't Edward come back here by himself? Couldn't he pick up the scent of his own paws and follow his trail to this room?"

"Not likely," replied Tom. "Our halls are filled with so many smells that his nose will grow confused. A cat who doesn't know this place is more likely to get lost."

"Not lost for good!" cried Checkers and Jenny.

"Let's hope not," said Tom. "But no matter what happens, you two must stay in your room. One cat on the loose is almost more than I can manage."

"We won't budge," they promised.

Tom lowered his nose and followed the scent of the runaway's trail along the floor from the door of 811 to a back stairway that was nearby. As the Royal did not have modern air conditioning, the doors of all stairways were propped open so that the air might circulate from floor to floor. Edward

had gone down these stairs!

"He was the mouse I heard earlier," thought Tom. "I should have caught him then, before he had a chance to go too far."

As Tom pursued the runaway's trail down one flight of stairs, and down another flight, and still another, he thought, "I hope Edward didn't grow frightened and run all the way down into the street. On those wild streets, a pet like Edward might get lost forever."

But Tom's nose discovered that at the

47

fourth-floor landing of the back stairway Edward had turned and entered the main hall of the Hotel.

"Good," thought Tom. "There may still be time for me to save him from those awful streets."

Edward, in fact, had spent much time in this part of the building. More than once he had left the main hall and wandered to the very end of some long passage. And for learning all this, Tom of the Royal had only his sniffer—his own little nose.

How weary the nose grew! But Tom followed the trail patiently hither and yon and finally back into the main hall and toward the elevator which was near the middle of the building. As he neared the elevator, its door creaked open and out swarmed a big group of travelers who were arriving late from some faraway land. Tom hid in a passage until the last of them had gone to their rooms.

When Tom returned to the main hall, he

found that those tourists had left behind
them a cloud of peppery smells brought
with them from the distant land they had
visited. By the time Tom had worked his
way through these stinging odors, his nose
was sore and useless.

"I'll try my ears," thought poor Tom. And
he cocked his ears and listened, but received
no news of Edward.

"Whiskers next," thought Tom. And he
perked his whiskers. *Flicker, flicker, flick*
. . . A radar message reached him that his
Lady, Mrs. Wilkins, was waiting for him at
the other end of the building, down at their
meeting place on the second-floor landing

of the grand stairway, near the abandoned ballroom.

"It's past midnight. I mustn't keep my Lady waiting any longer," Tom decided. "I'll go down to her and explain what's happened. Maybe she's seen Edward. If she hasn't, I'll come up here again and continue my search."

The prospect of a meeting, however brief, with his dear Lady, began to revive Tom's strength. And when he arrived at the grand stairway, his nose quivered slightly, as if Edward might have been here. Tom cocked his ears but heard no sound of Edward. He perked his whiskers. Ah! *Flicker, flicker, flick* . . . Edward was in the ballroom.

Now that the runaway had been found and all but caught, Tom grew angry. Edward had caused such trouble. Edward had made Tom keep Mrs. Wilkins waiting . . . "Oh, when I lay my paws on Edward . . ."

Tom sped down the grand stairway. As he drew near his Lady, he shouted through the banister, "Sorry to be late. A cat from 811 is on the loose. I only have to capture him and drive him to his room. Then I'll come back to you."

"Take your time, my dear," replied Mrs. Wilkins in a singsong voice.

Tom rushed to the ballroom door, which was partly open. He stood on the threshold and peered into the great, darkish, empty room, which contained no hiding place and no furniture except the grand piano. Street lights and moonlight filtered through the dusty windows while nothing moved upon the floor. Nothing stirred in any corner. But near a window in a far-off corner, on the flat lid of the piano, sat Edward.

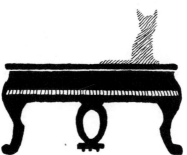

"On our grand piano, the finest property of the Royal," muttered the Hotel Cat. "Oh, when I get hold of Edward, I'll . . ."

Tom's fur bristled. He arched his back and made ready to spring forward. But a skirt came rustling behind him.

"Tom, let's keep an open mind. Let's wait and see what happens," said Mrs. Wilkins.

How They Might Become Friends Forever

The voice of Mrs. Wilkins calmed the anger of the Hotel Cat. He stood quietly with his Lady in the doorway and watched to see what Edward would do. Edward did nothing. Edward continued to sit as motionless as a lamppost, on top of the piano. He gave no sign of noticing that anyone was standing in the doorway. At last, however, he climbed carefully down onto the piano keys and began to walk on them—*tinkle–fa–re–mi–sol–la–tinkle–tinkle* . . .

Tom had never heard music from that old piano. He had never heard any piano music. Edward's melody was not so sweet as Mrs. Wilkins' little songs, yet it was music, and Tom liked it. He glanced at his Lady.

"Ah!" she exclaimed. "It's so long since we've had music in our ballroom."

But music or no music, the Hotel Cat had a job to do.

"Edward, come here!" he called firmly.

"Tom, is that you?" replied a dreamy voice.

Edward pattered to the doorway, and Tom now had his first good view of the guest who had caused so much trouble. Edward was a handsome, strong, young tiger cat, just about Tom's age. But Edward's eyes were filled with such a faraway look that Tom did not know quite what to say, though something needed to be said.

"Edward," he began, "you oughtn't to have left your room."

"My nose got the best of me," said Edward. "It made me want to find out more about this hotel—"

"Your Hotel Cat could have told you the history of the Royal," interrupted Tom.

". . . So I went sniffing here and there," continued Edward, in that same dreamy voice. "I wandered everywhere—I don't know where—until I came to this big room."

"The old grand ballroom of the Royal," said Tom.

"The musty smells in here," said Edward, "are the most wonderful of all."

"Flowers and satin slippers," murmured Mrs. Wilkins. "I can remember the days when there was music and dancing in this ballroom."

Edward gazed at Mrs. Wilkins and showed no surprise that she spoke perfect cat talk.

"Yes," he continued, "I could see people

twirling around like ghosts. And, after a while, the ballroom itself seemed like a ghost—and so did the piano, until I played the keys to make sure it was real. Then I could see cats dancing."

"Ghost cats?" asked Tom, feeling here was something the Hotel Cat ought to know about.

"No, Tom, those cats were real," said Edward, "and you were dancing with them."

"I never danced here in my life," protested Tom. And he wondered how he could bring a cat like this one to his senses. Mrs. Wilkins would be of little help. She seemed, at this moment, to be as foggy as Edward, though she was careful to keep a good hold on Tom's package of midnight snacks.

"See here, Edward," Tom said in a sharp voice, "your family wants you. Your master, Captain Tinker, has been searching for you everywhere—and with rheumatism in his legs."

"Rheumatism!" cried Edward, snapping

out of his fog and coming to attention. "I must go straight to my room."

"I'll take you there," said Tom.

"Thanks, Tom, but you needn't bother with me," said Edward. "I guess I can follow my own scent back to 811."

"Fat chance of that," declared Tom. "I'll go with you."

Then Mrs. Wilkins spoke up, saying, "I'll go, too, and wait until someone opens the door for Edward."

"Thank you, ma'am," said Edward.

"My Lady's name is Mrs. Wilkins," said Tom. "Mrs. Wilkins is a guest of our Hotel."

"What a lot of trouble I've caused everyone," sighed Edward.

"Now," thought the Hotel Cat, "now's my chance to give the runaway the scolding he deserves."

Tom looked straight at Edward but could not find the words to scold him. Edward was a cat like Tom, with a furry body, four paws, and a proud tail. And, oh, this Edward was so warm and friendly that Tom, who had never had a cat friend, took a step toward him. Edward took a step toward Tom. Then the grey and white Hotel Cat and the tiger guest touched noses, as a sign of friendship.

Tom and Edward stood together in the doorway of the ballroom, enjoying the sweet smell of one another's fur and saying nothing.

It was Mrs. Wilkins who broke the silence. "Tom, my dear," said she, "we really should take Edward to his family."

"Yes, of course," replied Tom. But to himself he sadly thought, "Oh, why does Edward have to have a family?"

As the little rescue group moved toward

the elevator, Tom went on thinking to himself, "That family will take Edward from me." And as the group rode up in the elevator, Tom knew he was being carried toward the time when he would have to part from his new friend. And while they all walked through the eighth-floor hall toward Edward's room, Tom hoped the door would not be opened right away. He'd like to have one last moment with his friend before they parted—perhaps forever.

But when Mrs. Wilkins tapped at the door, it was opened immediately by a tall gentleman who seemed to have just come in from a wearisome search.

"Is this Captain Tinker?" asked Mrs. Wilkins.

The gentleman nodded.

"Captain," she continued, "I am Mrs. Wilkins. Tom, our Hotel Cat, found Edward in the ballroom and has brought him home."

The Captain looked down at the two cats, gave a sigh of relief, and said, "Tom, a job well done. I thank you."

Edward also thanked Tom—thanked him with all his heart—and he thanked Mrs. Wilkins. Then, after looking up at his master as if to beg forgiveness, he skipped through the doorway and behind the door and disappeared into the room.

"And that's the end of Edward," thought poor Tom.

But it was not the end of Captain Tinker, who remained in the doorway, talking with Mrs. Wilkins. They were using human speech, of course, yet Tom continued to understand everything that Mrs. Wilkins said. Captain Tinker's voice was a different matter. Not all the Captain's words came through clearly to Tom, but the sound of them was pleasant, and much of their meaning could be understood.

The Captain was inviting Mrs. Wilkins and Tom to come into the room and meet the other two cats, Checkers and Jenny, who seemed very happy about their brother Edward's return.

Mrs. Wilkins replied, "No thank you, Captain, Tom and I will not come in. We would not care to intrude upon a family reunion. But nothing delights me more than the faces of happy cats. Might I take a peek?"

The Captain opened wide the door, and Mrs. Wilkins moved into the doorway. She stood in such a manner that Tom, if he wished, might find a place beside her.

Tom did not feel particularly interested in looking at the family which had robbed him of Edward. However, he decided that, as the Hotel Cat, he ought to see whether or not they kept their room tidy. So he stepped into the doorway and glanced about the big bright room. Everything was in such perfect order he never would have guessed a family of three young cats lived in it. But there they were, and he could not help noticing them.

The three were standing near their scratching post, and they were gazing from Tom to Mrs. Wilkins and back to Tom. He, in his turn, gazed at them and observed that older brother Edward was the only one with tiger stripes. Brother Checkers' fur was patterned fancily in black and white. Little sister Jenny was entirely black, except that in her shy face there glowed two eyes, like balls of light.

Mrs. Wilkins and Captain Tinker had stopped talking. The room was now so silent you could have heard a feather drop. "Somebody," thought Tom, "should say something."

"Tom"—it was little Jenny who was speaking, and her voice, though small, was very firm—"Tom, after what you've done for Edward, we three cats will be your friends forever."

Tom could scarcely believe his ears.

Checkers, however, repeated the words. "Friends forever."

And Edward echoed them, adding in his gentle, steady voice, "Tom, if you find time to call on us tomorrow night, we'll all be here. I promise."

"OK. I'll come," said Tom.

Then Mrs. Wilkins said to Captain Tinker, "Tom and I must bid you good night.

Tom has yet to eat his midnight snack. Edward may be hungry, too."

As Tom accompanied Mrs. Wilkins to the elevator, those joyful words—"friends forever"—rang in his head, lifted his heart, and made him feel he was walking on air. But as he rode down in the elevator with his Lady, a sorrowful thought began to trouble him, and as he walked beside her toward their meeting place, he grew more and more troubled.

After they had seated themselves on the landing of the old grand stairway, near the ballroom where so much had recently occurred, Tom ate his tidbits (chopped beef) in silence. Then he wiped his mouth and whiskers very slowly, and finally, as was often his custom when he had something difficult to say, he began in an easy, roundabout way.

"Did you see that toy?" he asked.

"Which toy, my dear?"

"That little shiny one dangling from the

top of their scratching post."

"Yes, my dear, I saw the toy."

Tom said, "It's a nifty scratching post."

"A good, strong scratching post," agreed his Lady.

Tom went on to say, "I saw they brought their own cat blankets, too."

"My dear, I believe that Captain Tinker's family will be with us for quite a while," said Mrs. Wilkins.

"But not forever," declared Tom, in the wise voice of a Hotel Cat who has learned how cat guests come and go.

Mrs. Wilkins said nothing to this, but stroked his head between his ears while waiting for him to come to the point.

"Some day," he murmured, "the Captain's cats will get a new boiler and go home. Some night I'll go upstairs and find them gone. Now tell me, how can we be friends forever?"

"Tom," she said, "those three cats looked to me like very honest cats. I believe they

meant what they said. I am sure that wherever they go, they will try to keep in touch
with you."

"How can they?" he asked.

Mrs. Wilkins answered, "Maybe their
master, Captain Tinker, will help them.
But, of course, a lot depends on you."

"What can I do?" demanded Tom.

"Ah, my dear," said Mrs. Wilkins, "you
have made great steps forward in your hotel
work and gathered power into your paws.
Use your power wisely in your work and
with your friends, and in the end it may help
all of you to become friends forever."

Cats in Every
Nook and Cranny

All next day, while he moused and ratted in the cellar, Tom thought happily of his three new friends in their room far, far above him. Those young cats in 811—Edward, Checkers, and Jenny—had indeed called themselves his "friends forever."

"And tonight, when I go up," he told himself, "and if I get to their door soon enough, maybe they'll invite me to come into their room. Maybe they'll let me try my claws on their scratching post."

So, after supper, Tom made ready to begin his night patrol much earlier than usual. He wished to allow plenty of time for anything that might delay him before he reached 811, which, of course, would be the last stop of his patrol. And he was glad he'd planned his time that way, because, just as he was about to climb the cellar stairs, there appeared on the landing above him a pair of big, dark, raggedy cats.

"Brother," they cried, "could you lend us a boiler?"

"Tramps at the Royal!" thought Tom in dismay. However, he remembered that not so long ago he himself had been a homeless street cat. He should at least give ear to the story of these strangers.

"Do you come in peace?" he asked.

"We spit no spit," they answered. And, as a matter of fact, they remained standing politely on the landing.

"Name your names," he said.

"Sinbad and The Duke," said they.

The pair spoke together, like old pals, and Tom did not bother to learn which one was Sinbad, and which The Duke.

"I'm Tom, the Hotel Cat. What brought you here?" he said.

"The wind," they answered. "Something in the wind told us the Royal was the place to go."

"And before you listened to the wind, where were you?" demanded Tom.

"Camping in the cellar of somebody's little house."

"Were you asked to leave?" continued Tom.

"No, the old boiler busted. We couldn't find another decent one. So we trotted over to the Royal. There's snow in our ears and ice between our toes."

"Is it that cold outside?" asked Tom.

"Brother, it's the Winter of the Big Freeze. Step outdoors, and you'll hear the boilers busting."

Tom said, "My hotel work keeps me indoors day and night." And then he added, "Work has its advantages." But Tom wasn't trying to give the two idlers a lecture. He was thinking to himself, "It lies within my power to provide these tramps with shelter. But first I ought to make a few rules clear to them."

So he asked them, "Are you hungry?"

"Not now. On our way over, we snitched a lamb chop from a meat store."

"Fellas," said Tom, "I know such things happen out there on the streets. But if I should let you stay at the Royal, there would have to be no snitching."

"No snitching, we promise," they replied.

"And if you stayed here," Tom continued, "there would have to be no wandering all over the Hotel."

"No wandering, we promise."

But Tom remarked, "There are promises and promises. How do you make a promise?"

"On the honor of our paws 'n claws. And if we break a promise, chop them off," cried Sinbad and The Duke.

They had given the solemn oath of tramp cats, and the young Hotel Cat could not have asked for more.

"Fellas," he said, "I have a cozy office near our new boiler. You may share my office and whatever food I get until the Big Freeze ends."

"Brother!" they cried. And they rushed down the cellar stairs so joyfully that Tom feared those tramps were going to hug him. But they stopped in front of him and demanded, "Does your office have a toilet?"

"My office has a bed, a box with wooden sides for sharpening the claws, and a plastic box containing newspapers for the purpose which you mention."

"The toilet first," they begged. "We're in an awful hurry."

Tom ushered Sinbad and The Duke to the doorway of his office. "Go in," he said, "and make yourselves at home."

As the tramps scurried toward the plastic box, he called after them, "Don't leave the office."

"OK," they answered.

Tom said, "I'm off to the upper floors. I work there in the halls at night."

"Get back before the milkman comes," shouted Sinbad and The Duke from the plastic box.

Though the arrival of the tramps had considerably delayed Tom, he hoped that a quick patrol of the floors above would enable him to make up his lost time. He still looked forward to calling at the door of his friends in 811 early enough to be invited into their room for a little get-together. But as he made his rounds from floor to floor, he discovered that in at least one room on every floor there was a new cat guest who required his attention.

These guests were safe under lock and key behind the closed doors of their rooms, but Tom, of course, had to stop at each door and deliver his friendly Welcome Speech. The Speech—alas!—did not calm the guests. It stirred them up and gave them a chance to delay him further with their chatter. He had got no higher than the fifth floor when midnight came and went. Thus, as he neared the end of this hall and found himself close to the old grand stairway, he decided, "I ought not keep my Lady waiting. I'll see her now, and after that, I'll do the three top floors and 811."

Tom zipped down the stairway to the second floor, joined Mrs. Wilkins at their meeting place, and wailed, "My Lady, what a night! Cats have been arriving like a flock of pigeons. They've been settling into every

nook and cranny of the Royal."

"Ah!" said Mrs. Wilkins. "That's what Mr. Peter meant when he passed me earlier."

"What did Mr. Peter say?" asked Tom.

"He said you were doing splendidly, which is high praise indeed from a night watchman."

"Mr. Peter doesn't know half of it," muttered Tom. "He doesn't know the kind of high-geared pets I've had to manage. And in my office downstairs, guess what? I've taken in two tramps."

Mrs. Wilkins patted Tom and spread out his tidbits (cold duck), which he ate hungrily. Then he went on to say, "Such chatterers. I mean these high-geared ones I've just been welcoming upstairs. They'd have talked my head off if I'd let them, which I didn't. And still, I've gone no higher than the fifth floor."

"Tom, what did they talk about?"

"Themselves and why they came to us and where they came from. They all are cases of broken boilers and come from some little old houses near a garden down the way. Did you ever hear of any such houses?"

"Yes, Tom, I have heard there is a group of them not far from here—houses which, like the Royal, have escaped the bulldozer."

"My Lady, did you ever hear of something called the Cat Club?"

"Yes, Tom. That is to say, I have read about the Cat Club in stories."

"But that Club, or part of it, is here right now in our Hotel," groaned Tom. "And those darling pets I've been telling you about are members of that crazy Club."

"Ah!" said Mrs. Wilkins thoughtfully.

"And they'll be the death of me with all their chatter," added Tom. "Wretches! Why did they have to pick tonight for coming? Tonight's the night I'd planned to make a rather special call on 811. Oh, woe is me! What shall I do?"

"My dear, continue to do the best you can, and it may end in something pleasant for everyone to remember," replied Mrs. Wilkins.

Mrs. Wilkins, as if unwilling to keep Tom any longer, rose and let him escort her to her room. Then he dashed up to the sixth floor to resume his patrol.

It was now too late for him to expect he would be invited into the room of his friends in 811. By the time he reached their door, at the end of his patrol, their master, Captain Tinker, would have gone to bed. But Tom did hope that Edward, Checkers, and Jenny would be waiting for him at their side of the door. Hadn't those three cats declared themselves to be his "friends forever"? "And 'friends forever' ought to mean," he reasoned, "that they'd sit up for me, even if I'm late—though not too late."

But on the sixth floor, Tom had to stop at a door and welcome another member of the Cat Club. And it grew later. And there was another member—another of those chatterers—on the seventh floor. And it grew still later.

And on the eighth, or top, floor, behind the door of a room near the landing of the grand stairway, Tom discovered two more cats who belonged to the Club. Luckily for him, these two had just arrived. They had not quite recovered from their trip and were, in fact, still locked in their traveling baskets. Tom cut short their chatter by saying, "I hope that when you have a chance to look about your room you will find everything to your liking."

Then Tom scurried down the hall on the last lap of his patrol, and here nothing further delayed him. As he drew near 811, he could see a light gleaming through the crack between the closed door and the floor. His heart leapt. "Oh, ho!" he thought. "They're all sitting up for me. That's what it is to have friends forever."

But suddenly his whiskers twitched, his nose quivered. Edward, Checkers, and Jenny had a visitor! Another cat—a brand new cat—was with them. What a blow to Tom! "So much for friends forever," he sighed. "It doesn't take them long to find someone else to keep them company."

Tom felt like walking past 811 without stopping. But 811 was part of his patrol, and he should at least inquire about Captain Tinker's health. For, though human guests weren't usually Tom's business, Captain Tinker was one of those people who, like Mrs. Wilkins, became very much the business of a Hotel Cat.

So Tom pulled up at the door of 811, and in his most courteous voice said, "Good evening."

"Hi, Tom! Hi! Hi! We've been waiting ages for you," replied Edward, Checkers, and Jenny from a point close to their side of the door. And their voices could not have sounded more friendly.

"How's Captain Tinker's rheumatism?" asked Tom.

"Better and almost gone," they answered.

And the next moment the Captain himself opened the door and said to Tom, "Come in."

More About
the Cat Club

Tom, who could not say No to Captain Tinker's coaxing voice, stepped into the bright room. Jenny had dressed up for the new cat and was wearing a red scarf. Except for the scarf and the new cat, nothing had changed. Jenny and her brothers greeted Tom again as if they were indeed his trusty friends.

The newcomer, whom Tom had expected to dislike, had a pleasant manner, and while waiting for an introduction, stood politely to one side. Tom noted that he was somewhat older than the other three, and that his fur, which was white except for a thatch of grey worn like a cap between the ears, had a windswept look. Who could he be?

Edward said to Tom, "This is Jack Tar, Ship's Cat aboard the good ship *Sea Queen*. Once we sailed around the world with Jack. Since then, he spends his shore leave with us."

"A sailor cat," thought Tom, eyeing Jack with greater interest.

Then Jack stepped forward, saying in a hearty voice, "Tom, I'm pleased to meet you. My young friends have told me all about you."

"Oh!" stammered Tom, surprised and

happy that he had not been overlooked in conversation. Then he raised his voice, and in his finest hotel manner said, "Jack **Tar**, welcome to the Royal Hotel."

"Thanks," said Jack. "It's good to be here."

"Rough trip?" asked Tom.

"We had a hard time bringing the *Sea Queen* through the wind and ice of New York Harbor," replied Jack.

Tom thought to himself, "Here's a cat who knows what work is. Those other guests I've been welcoming tonight are quite a different sort." And, aloud, he said to Jack, "When did your ship come into port?"

"We docked this afternoon. Captain Tinker was on hand to bring me here."

A brief pause in the conversation followed, but Captain Tinker did what should be done. He spread a clean smooth newspaper on the floor near the scratching post, and on the paper he placed little piles of catnip leaves—a pile for each cat. Afterward, he retired to a corner of the room, sat down in his armchair, lit his pipe, and left the five cats to their own world of happenings.

Catnip, which loosens a cat's tongue and enlivens a cat's spirit, was a rare treat for Tom. He took one sniff at his tickly-smelling pile, rolled twice across his section of the newspaper, sat up, and raised his ears to show he was ready for more conversation.

Jack said to him, "Your hotel strikes me as very shipshape."

"No," protested Tom, "it's bursting at the seams."

"More cats, I'll bet," cried Checkers brightly.

"More than I would care to mention," replied Tom.

"Busted boilers?" asked Checkers.

Tom nodded.

"Busted where?" demanded Checkers.

"In some little old houses near a garden down the way," answered Tom, hoping that this piece of information would satisfy the Bright One.

But Checkers said, "Our master's house is down the way. Maybe it's the same way. Come on, Tom, tell us who the new cats are. Maybe we know some of them."

"Guests at my Hotel," objected Tom, "are entitled to their privacy. I don't like to carry news about them to other guests."

"Tom, those of us in 811 aren't just ordinary guests. We're your friends," argued Checkers. "And we'd be interested in anything you care to tell us. Jack Tar would be especially interested. He's been months and months at sea without a.wiggle of cat news from New York."

Jack looked at Tom and remarked, "True enough, true enough. And news of land affairs is always welcome to a sailor cat."

The words of the Ship's Cat swayed the

young Hotel Cat, who replied, "I suppose there's no harm in mentioning a few names from our guest list."

"Name all the names, from floor to floor. Jack would like to hear everything there is to hear," urged Checkers.

Tom took a whiff of catnip and then said, "OK. On the second floor, where the guest rooms start, we have a cat named Concertina. She's Secretary of something called the Cat Club. Did you ever hear of such a thing?"

His listeners nodded quietly, and Checkers said, "Go on."

Tom took another whiff of catnip and continued. "On the third floor, there's a Persian cat, named Madame Butterfly, who brought along her nose flute. She told me the flute was still packed away in her traveling kit. I hope it stays there."

Checkers laughed and said to Tom, "But if some night you hear a toot, you'll know it comes from the flute of the Club's most beautiful member."

"I hope to hear no toots," declared Tom.

"Go on," urged Checkers.

"On the fourth floor, together in one room but rather well-behaved, are young Romulus and Remus."

"Twin cats, who comfort each other," explained Checkers. "Please go on."

"On the fifth floor, in a room at one end of the main hall, we have a cat named Arabella, who wants to know if a cat named Antonio has turned up here. As a matter of fact, Antonio is in a room at the other end of the hall, dying for news of Arabella."

Checkers giggled and said, "Those two are the Club's sweethearts."

Tom looked sharply at Master Checkers and demanded, "How come you know so much about the members of this Cat Club?"

"Because," replied Checkers, "the Club meets at night, weather permitting, in the garden of our master, Captain Tinker. Please go on."

"On the sixth floor, we have a happy-sounding cat who jumps around his room. I had to beg him to leave the walls standing."

"Macaroni, the Club's fancy dancer," said Checkers.

"On the seventh floor," continued Tom, "we have a fellow with a squeaky voice, who needs wire and screws."

"Solomon, the inventor, who's making a television set for the Club," explained Checkers. "Oh, do go on."

"Here on your own floor, in a room at the other end of this hall, and not yet out of their traveling baskets when I passed by, are a young nephew and his uncle. The nephew is Junior. The uncle is—"

"Our President! Our Club President is here!" exclaimed the cats of 811.

"*Your* President. So you are members of this Cat Club," stammered Tom.

"Yes," said Checkers, "Edward, Jenny, and I are regular members. Jack Tar is an honorary member."

"Honorary only means," Jack interrupted, "that I come to meetings whenever I can."

Then little Jenny spoke up, saying in her shy voice, "Tom, aren't you happy that you could help so many of us get in out of the cold?"

"It's a pleasant side of hotel work," he admitted. "But enough's enough. No more of you to come, I hope."

Jenny replied, "The Club has four other members. One is Pickles, the Fire Cat, who lives with his firemen at Hook and Ladder Company 7X of the New York City Fire Department."

Tom said quickly, "Well, we don't have to worry about Pickles."

"And Florio is with his mistress in sunny Florida," said Jenny.

"Nor worry about him," said Tom.

"But the other two," continued Jenny in a sad voice, "the other two have no home. They have neither master nor mistress to bring them to a warm spot. There's absolutely nobody to help Sinbad and The Duke."

Tom thought to himself in great astonishment, "So those two tramps down in my office are members of this fancy Club."

However, he remained silent. He was now enjoying the importance of being the Hotel

Cat—the one and only cat who knew everything that happened at the Royal. Though
he was very fond of little Jenny, he felt it
would be fun to keep her waiting just a moment before he surprised her with his bit of
news.

So he said to her in a careless voice, "If
those two fellas you mentioned have no
home, maybe it's their own fault. Maybe
Sinbad and The Duke are too rough to live
in anybody's house."

"Tom, maybe the right person never invited them to come in at the right time," replied Jenny. "Anyway, Sinbad and The
Duke have learned to live on their own.
They manage quite well in good weather,
and when it's cold, they creep into somebody's cellar. But boiler after boiler has been
bursting. What if their boiler burst too?"

"It did," said Tom.

"How do you know? Oh, tell us what you
know!" begged Jenny.

Tom lowered his head to the newspaper

on the floor, took a good long whiff of catnip, raised his head, and began, "Tonight, just as I was about to leave my office, two strange cats arrived at the cellar door. I asked them, 'Do you come in peace?' 'We spit no spit,' said they. I told them, 'Name your names.' And they said, 'Sinbad and The Duke.' "

"Sinbad and The Duke!" exclaimed Jenny. "Where are they now?"

Tom brushed a bit of catnip from his whiskers, removed another bit of catnip from his back, raised his head very slowly, and then said, "Guests downstairs in my office."

"Tom, what a happy, happy ending!" cried Jenny.

"And how well the tale was told," said Edward.

Tom had indeed told his story so well that it seemed to round off the catnip party. But he felt obliged to say another word to his companions. "Listen," he began, "I haven't had time to tell Sinbad and The Duke that the rest of you are staying at the Royal. And I don't intend to tell them or any of our upstairs guests. I can't have guests leaving their rooms to pay calls on one another. So will the four of you promise to let nothing of what I've told you travel beyond 811?"

The Ship's Cat answered, "I promise on the honor of my sailor's cap." And he lowered his head so that all might see the thatch of grey fur which grew between his ears.

"I promise on the honor of this paw of mine which writes my poems," said Edward.

"I promise on the honor of my tongue which asks so many questions," said Checkers.

"I promise on the honor of the bright red

scarf my master knit for me," said Jenny.

Tom stood up, declaring, "I hate to leave this pleasant party."

The others accompanied him to the door. But before Captain Tinker had time to open it, Jenny said to Tom, "Just a moment. I've been thinking . . ."

Jenny's voice sounded as if she'd had another of her long, deep thoughts. So Tom said quickly, "Can it wait?"

"Yes, Tom, it can wait until tomorrow night, but not much longer. Promise us that you will call at 811 tomorrow night. Make it a solemn promise."

"OK, I'll come," said Tom. "I promise on the honor of my white shirt front."

No sooner had Tom said those words than Captain Tinker opened the door. Tom thanked the Captain for the lovely catnip, and everybody said, "Farewell until tomorrow night."

Tom took a shortcut to the cellar by means of the back stairway. But he paused

at every landing, glanced up and down the hall, cocked his ears, widened his nose, and twitched his whiskers. All seemed peaceful. A stranger would never have guessed that members of the Cat Club were occupying rooms from the top floor to the cellar of the Royal.

The cellar, too, was calm. Not a speck of dust had been disturbed. Sinbad and The

Duke had kept their promise. They had remained in his office, though when he got there, they were almost falling through the doorway.

"Brother," they moaned, "we thought you'd never come."

"I've had a busy night," he answered.

"What kind of work do you do upstairs?" they asked.

"Hotel work," he said.

"Such as—" said they.

"What any good hotel cat ought to do," replied Tom. "Tonight I've had a pawful."

Tom suddenly felt very tired.

"Listen, fellas, in the morning we can talk," he murmured. "Right now my brains are sinking. Let me go to sleep."

"OK," said Sinbad and The Duke.

Tom jumped up on his bed, lay down, and curled himself into a comfortable position. His two guests joined him, but they did not lie down. They brought their noses close to his. He shut his eyes and wrapped his tail across his face. The noses of his guests moved to his back. And just before he drifted off to sleep, he heard Sinbad and The Duke say softly to each other, "Tom's had a roll in Captain Tinker's catnip."

Learning the Sailor's Hornpipe

While Tom slept, he had a dream. He dreamed that the news had got around that the tramp cats, Sinbad and The Duke, who had arrived earlier in the night, were staying in his office. And he went on dreaming that some of the upstairs members of the Cat Club—not the cats in 811, but others whom he did not know—were escaping from their rooms and rushing down and entering his office to say Hello to his two guests.

Tom awoke with a start, expecting trouble. But he found his office empty except for the tramps, who were sitting close beside him on the bed, with their noses again on his back.

"Get off my fur. I want to get up," ordered Tom.

Sinbad and The Duke lifted their noses.

"Tom," they said, speaking together as was their custom, "we've sniffed up and down your coat. It smells of more than Captain Tinker's catnip. It smells of the Captain's three cats, and the sailor cat, Jack Tar. Are they upstairs?"

"Who is this Captain Tinker?" asked Tom, as if he'd never met the gentleman. For, after the dream, Tom was more determined than ever to keep mum about the Cat Club. He didn't wish to tempt Sinbad and The Duke into slipping away from the cellar and roaming through the upstairs halls to visit friends.

"The Captain's a retired sea captain, has a house that has a garden—garden's used by cats for meetings," said Sinbad and The Duke.

"Who are those cats?" asked Tom in a careless voice.

"Oh, just a Cat Club," replied Sinbad and The Duke. And they would say no more. Apparently they did not wish to boast about being members of a Club to which Tom did not belong.

Tom, at this moment, wouldn't have given one spit to be a member of that Club. He had other things to think about, such as breakfast. Mr. Fred, the Furnace Man, could be heard stirring about in the cellar, and soon he entered the office with a saucer of breakfast for Tom. The sight of the two tramps caused Mr. Fred to gasp some words that sounded like "What have we here?"

As Mr. Fred understood very little of cat language, Tom replied by jumping down from the bed and weaving himself around the legs of his Boss and uttering some pitiful *meows*. Tom believed this was the clearest way of telling Mr. Fred "It's awfully, awfully, a-w-f-u-l-l-y cold outside. Sinbad and The Duke are friends of mine. Their boiler burst. Please may they stay with me until the Big Freeze is over?"

Fortunately, Mr. Fred had a kind heart, which helps in figuring out what cats are trying to say. He muttered something about "Yes, if your pals keep out of mischief." Then he shuffled away and returned with a large platter of enough good canned food for all three cats. As he set the platter on the floor, they thanked him with purrs and wavings of the tail. By the time the platter had been licked clean, Mr. Fred had disappeared, and Tom was alone with his two guests.

Tom wiped his mouth and whiskers and

washed his grey coat. His tongue was on his white shirt front when he looked up at Sinbad and The Duke and said, "Don't you fellas ever wash?"

"Only in the evening," they replied.

"You're at the Royal now," said Tom.

Sinbad and The Duke grinned and passed their tongues across their dark speckled fur.

"That's better," observed Tom.

"What next?" they asked.

"Cellar work," he answered.

"We'll lend a helping paw," said they.

The three of them went hunting, and they peered down all the mouse holes and the rat holes in the cellar walls. But Tom had worked so well the day before that not a creature could be seen or heard.

After a while, the cats returned to the office, where Sinbad and The Duke again questioned Tom about the kind of work he did upstairs at night.

"I patrol the halls," he answered.

"For mice and rats?" they asked.

"And this and that," he added.

"This and that is what we'd like to hear about," said they. "Something tells us a lot is happening up there."

"My work on the floors above can have its busy moments," replied Tom in a voice that indicated he did not care to discuss the subject any further.

"Well," said Sinbad and The Duke, "there's not much work down here to do. Let's dance."

"Dance!" exclaimed Tom in a shocked tone. For, in his mind, it seemed wicked to dance during work hours, even when there was no work to be done.

"Come on, Tom, don't be a stiff. What dances do you know?" continued Sinbad and The Duke.

Poor Tom did not know any dances. So he said, "I'd rather sit. You two can do the dancing. But don't go beyond the office, and please, nothing rowdy."

"Elegantly, or not at all," laughed Sinbad and The Duke.

Tom was surprised at seeing how elegantly those big, rough-looking tramps did bow to one another and place themselves, like partners, side by side. Next they rose on their hind legs and capered daintily together around the office floor. And then, as softly as a feather falling, they dropped down again on all four paws.

"What was that dance?" asked Tom, who had not dreamed that such a thing existed.

"The sailor's hornpipe. It's a dance that's danced by sailor cats on ships at sea. We learned it in Captain Tinker's garden. Shall we teach you the steps?"

"OK," said Tom.

"Upsy-daisy!" cried his teachers.

The young Hotel Cat rose on his hind legs, lost his balance, toppled down, and hit the floor with his bottom.

"Try again," said Sinbad and The Duke. "And this time, shoot a front paw high above your head, as if you're trying to catch a fly. And let your paw stay up—to help you keep your balance."

Tom rose, waved a front paw in the air, and kept his balance.

"Now skip," they ordered.

Tom made a few plain skips across the floor, and for a cat who had not danced since he was a kitten, he did quite well. Next he learned some fancy steps, and as the day wore on, he became better and better at the hornpipe. He loved the fun of kicking at the floor and rising in the air. Sinbad and The Duke nicknamed him Mr. Twinkle Toes, and Tom felt he would do anything in the world for these two tramps who had brightened his life in the cellar.

But after supper, when it was time for him to leave for his upstairs patrol, and the tramps begged to go with him, Tom replied, "No, fellas, not tonight. Tonight I have to make a lot of business calls. But some night, if my work up there grows easier, I'd like to take you on a little tour of our Hotel. It would be a pity if you left the Royal without at least a glimpse of our old grand stairway and the ballroom."

Why the Club
Should Hold a Meeting

As Tom climbed the cellar stairs, he hoped the members of the Cat Club who had arrived the night before had by now settled down quietly in their rooms.

"Those rooms are far apart, beyond sound of one another," he thought. "And none of those guests seems to me to have the nose of a poet, which would take him wandering, like Edward. And none of them, I'm sure, is trained like me to detect each little thing that happens at this Hotel. So if I tell them nothing, they will never know their friends are here. And they'll not escape from rooms to look for one another. And everything will run smoothly, as it ought to—oughtn't it?—in a well-managed hotel."

Tom was still on the second floor, making the first stop of his patrol at the door of the Club Secretary, Concertina, and she was sighing, "How I wish I might have news for my Club records," when—

Toot-a-loo-a-loo . . . Music from somewhere reached Tom's ears.

"Tom!" cried Concertina, "Who's playing that nose flute?"

Tom, without stopping to reply, dashed toward the music. *Toot-a-loo-a-loo-a-loo.* It came from the third-floor landing of the grand stairway. Tom bounded to the landing, and there sat the Persian beauty, Madame Butterfly. The young Hotel Cat had never seen such long silvery fur. He had never seen a nose flute. But he could waste no time.

"Quiet, please," he ordered. "You'll wake up everyone."

"The night is just beginning," replied Madame Butterfly with a smile.

Toot-a-loo-a-loo-a . . .

Tom nipped the beauty's bottom and drove her to the door of her room. The door stood partly open, and Madame Butterfly knew perfectly well where she belonged. But she lingered in the doorway and gave another toot. A woman's voice inside the room said "Naughty Butterfly," and a hand pulled the lovely creature in and shut the door. Silence descended on the room.

The damage, however, had been done.

Other members of the Club had heard the tooting of the nose flute. As Tom went from floor to floor, he found these cats safe in their rooms, but in a state of great excitement.

"Who played that flute?" they asked him.

"When I have news for you, I'll let you know," said Tom politely.

Even the members in far-off rooms who had not heard the tooting were excited. They had caught something in the air, and they asked Tom, "What other cats are staying here?"

"When I have news for you, I'll let you know," Tom answered calmly, though he was growing more and more fearful that sooner or later his guests might go running through the halls to gather their own news.

Tom finally climbed the last flight of the grand stairway and approached the door of the Club President. The President, who had been confined in his traveling basket the night before, was now waiting close to his side of the door, like the more ordinary members. But his voice, though pleasant, was that of a Great One accustomed to asking questions—and receiving answers.

"Tom, are you having trouble?" he inquired.

"Nothing to speak of, sir," replied Tom, who had decided that this President was not his own President and therefore need not be told everything.

"Tom, if you do run into trouble, and if I can be of help," said the President, "feel free to call on me at any time of night. The President of a Cat Club never sleeps. And he sleeps least of all when the tooting of a nose flute, whose sweet tones he recognized, and a strange restlessness in the air have warned him that there may be trouble at the Royal."

Trouble at the Royal! Those words made poor Tom shiver. And as he hurried from the Presidential door, he thought that just as soon as he had finished his patrol he ought to have a good long talk with Mrs. Wilkins. Perhaps his Lady could tell him how to prevent cats from running all over the Hotel and maybe getting lost.

Fortunately, as Tom continued on this final lap of his patrol, he found no new cat guests, nor, during his rounds, had he detected any elsewhere in the Hotel. Furthermore, none, for a while, were likely to arrive. All vacant rooms had been filled by humans who apparently sought shelter from the Big Freeze. Some of these people had brought along their children, canary birds, and dogs. But that was not the business of the Hotel Cat. His only problem was the restless Cat Club.

Soon Tom reached the last stop of his patrol—the door of the four cats in 811. He had promised Jenny that he'd call on them tonight, and now he decided to remain on the outside just long enough to say Hello. The door, however, was quickly opened, and at Captain Tinker's invitation, Tom stepped into the room.

The four cats, gathering round him,

asked, "How are things with you?"

"Wild," he muttered. And briefly he described the events, from the tooting of the nose flute to the warning of their President.

"Oh, Tom!" exclaimed Jenny. "What you've been saying fits in with a little plan that we have. Our plan would keep the restless members quiet by giving them something to look forward to."

"Jenny, what do you mean?"

"Tom, last night when you were leaving us," replied Jenny, "I was thinking, and today all of us in 811 have been thinking, that the members of the Club really ought to get together. Could you arrange for a Club meeting?"

"No, no, no," protested Tom. "All of you together would blow the roof off."

"We wouldn't, Tom, because our President sees to it that our meetings are orderly. And really, Tom, our Club ought to meet to vote on special business that's come up at the Royal," said Jenny.

"I hope your Club has found no fault with the services of the Hotel Cat," stammered Tom.

"Oh, no," cried Jenny, in such a warm voice that Tom's mind was relieved on that point.

"Then, Jenny," he said, "I should think any other business could wait until the members get their new boilers and go home."

"No," insisted Jenny. "We ought to meet at the Royal on a night while Jack Tar is still with us. Jack likes to attend our meetings."

Tom, who admired the Ship's Cat, shot him a questioning glance.

"Quite true," said Jack. "I do enjoy Club meetings. And for me, a meeting at the

Royal would be something extra special—a night to remember during my lonely watches at sea. Yes, Tom, no matter where I sailed on the grey Atlantic or the blue Pacific, it would be a night to remember."

As the Ship's Cat spoke those last words, his voice held the sound of the whole great world, which the Hotel Cat might never see himself but where his Hotel might be remembered. The thought stirred Tom's imagination. But after thinking seriously for a moment, he said, "This Club of yours has so many members that I could never find a place for all of you to meet in."

"Tom, what about the old grand ballroom of the Royal?" asked Edward softly.

"The old grand ballroom of the Royal!" exclaimed Tom, whose imagination was further stirred by this suggestion. But he felt obliged to say, "Our ballroom floor is covered with dust."

"Stardust," murmured Edward dreamily.

"Stardust!" echoed Tom. "Why, that's

116

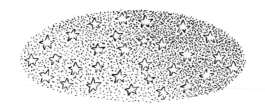

what Mrs. Wilkins calls it. I'll have to talk this over with my Lady."

"And tell your Lady"—it was Checkers, the Bright One, who was speaking—"tell her that after our business meeting, we'd like to dance the sailor's hornpipe."

"Not so fast, young cat," said Tom.

But Checkers pushed ahead with plans and named the whole affair the Stardust Ball.

"Stardust Ball," repeated Tom. The words rolled pleasantly on his tongue, captured his imagination completely, and made everything seem possible.

"The Stardust Ball," continued Checkers, "should be held on the first night of the full moon, which is the last night before Jack Tar returns to the sea. We have no time to lose. Will you speak with Mrs. Wilkins right away, and if she says Yes, will you go and try to get the OK of our President and then bring us the news?"

"What sort of fellow is your President?" asked Tom.

"Our President is a cat who likes big plans," replied Checkers, as he shoved Tom to the door.

The Manager of
a Truly Grand Affair

It's up to me," thought the young Hotel Cat as he hastened down the back stairs to seek the help of Mrs. Wilkins. "And if I use my head, I can give the Cat Club a night to remember."

Tom found his Lady sitting at their meeting place, on the second-floor landing of the grand stairway, near the ballroom. She did not seem surprised that he came late. But he said to her, "I'm sorry. The thing is—"

"My dear, eat what I have brought you and then tell me."

119

Mrs. Wilkins unfolded his package.

"Shrimps, three shrimps!" he cried, and ate them gratefully, because three shrimps are supposed to be a good-luck sign for cats. Then he murmured, "Imagine our old deserted ballroom brought to life with a real Ball."

She clapped her little hands delightedly, and as he described the plans for the Stardust Ball, she let her thoughts wander, as if in a dream. But he called her back to attention with a gentle poke of the paw.

"There's a problem," he whispered. "We'll have to get permission for the Club to use the ballroom. Could you help?"

"My dear," replied Mrs. Wilkins, "I have lived a long time at the Royal, and my word here carries weight. I shall ask the Hotel owner to allow the Club to meet in the ball-room. I can promise you his answer will be Yes."

"Thank you, my Lady," cried Tom, feeling happy that he had brought arrangements to this point. "Now I must get the OK of the Club President."

"Ah, Tom, the sooner you do that the better because the first night of the full moon is only three nights away."

Mrs. Wilkins rose, and Tom escorted her to her room. Then he scampered up the grand stairway to get the President's OK.

The door of the Presidential room was closed; no light shone through the crack between the door and the floor, and somewhere, in a corner of the room, the President of the Cat Club, who liked big plans and claimed he never slept, was snoring.

"Oh," thought Tom, "he'll be hopping mad to have been caught napping. How shall I manage him?"

Tom scratched delicately at the door.

"Uncle, wake up!" cried a shrill young voice.

"Quiet, Junior. I'll take charge of this," said the President. And in a voice still somewhat drowsy, he called out, "Who's there?"

"It's Tom, sir, your Hotel Cat, who needs your opinion about some plans—some rather big plans."

"Big plans!" exclaimed the President. And he pattered quickly on his heavy paws to his side of the door and said in a brisk voice, "Tom, tell me everything."

So Tom told the President about the many members of the Cat Club who were staying at the Royal, and about the tooting of the nose flute, which, as the President himself had noted, had stirred up some restlessness. "And, sir, if you approve the plans," continued Tom, "a meeting of your Club might help the restless members to let off their steam."

"Tom, there should be a more solid reason

for a meeting," objected the President.

"Sir, there is, or at least Jenny thinks there is. She thinks your Club should vote on special business that's come up at the Royal. I don't know what the business is, though Jenny did say there would be no complaints about the services of the Hotel Cat."

"Tom, your services are excellent," declared the President. Then the President remained silent, as if putting his great mind to work, and next he gave a mysterious chuckle and finally, in a serious voice, he said, "Pray continue."

While Tom unfolded the plans for the Stardust Ball, the President paced to and fro along his side of the door. And as the plans grew bigger, so did the President seem to grow bigger and bigger.

When Tom described how a Lady, Mrs. Wilkins, a human of the very highest rank, who had long been a guest at the Royal, would be able to obtain permission for the Club to use the grand ballroom, the President stopped his pacing, and his great mind seemed to fill the room. But Tom had no way of guessing what went on inside that Presidential mind.

At last the President cleared his throat. "Tom," he said in a most gracious voice, "when you have a chance, will you please convey my compliments to your Lady? Tell her also that I believe Captain Tinker would help wherever possible, and that at our Club meeting I myself would enforce order. However, Tom, I should insist that you, as our Hotel Cat, attend our meeting, just to see that nothing does get out of paw."

"I would attend," said Tom.

"Then, Tom, with your help the Cat Club shall hold a Stardust Ball," declared the President.

"Thank you, sir, and if that is all—"

"No, Tom. I have a few plans of my own for those cats in 811. Our sailor cat, Jack Tar, may rest from his voyage, so as to be in shape to dance a lively hornpipe. The others, however, have work to do. Jenny is to prepare a speech about the business on which the Club must vote. She may make her speech short and plain and to the point and

125

deliver it herself at the business meeting. And Edward is to write a poem that will dress up that meeting. As for Checkers, he is to help you with social arrangements, such as getting out the invitations."

"Checkers!" exclaimed Tom. And he was on the point of adding that the Royal Hotel was very old and famous and that Master Checkers was rather young—and sometimes hasty.

But the President, as if looking through the door and straight into the thoughts of the Hotel Cat, said, "Tom, give Checkers a chance. He has a social touch—a social paw."

"I'll keep an open mind," said Tom. And as he hurried from the Presidential door, he thought to himself, "So far, so good. Here's hoping Master Checkers doesn't throw a fish bone into things."

When Tom reached 811, he found that Captain Tinker had gone to bed, but the four cats were waiting at their side of the door.

"What news?" they asked.

"The Stardust Ball is in the bag," he said.

"You wonder cat!" they cried.

Tom then gave them details of his talks with Mrs. Wilkins and the President. But not until the very end did he tell Checkers, "You're to help me with social arrangements."

"Tom," replied Checkers in a modest voice. "I've already thought of what an invitation to the Ball ought to say. But, of course, I need to know what you think. You're the Boss."

The word "Boss" was spoken with such respect that Tom softened toward his young assistant and said, "Shoot."

And Checkers began, *The President of the Cat Club cordially invites the members . . .*

"Not bad," murmured Tom, whose ears, in fact, were charmed by the sound of those smoothly flowing words.

"To a Stardust Ball to be held in the

Grand Ballroom of the Royal Hotel . . ."

"Better and better," said Tom.

"From midnight until dawn . . ."

"The best of hours," said Tom.

"On the first night of the full moon . . ."

"The best of nights," said Tom.

"Brief business meeting to be followed with the sailor's hornpipe," concluded Checkers.

"The best of invitations, and quite worthy of the Royal," declared Tom.

"Tom, can you remember it?"

"Word for word," replied Tom.

And before you could have said "whiskers," Tom had received from Checkers a couple of little messages for Sinbad and  The Duke and was speeding down the back stairs toward his office. He could hardly wait to deliver an invitation to the two tramps, who were penned in the cellar.

Sinbad and The Duke greeted him mournfully and wailed, "Why won't you tell us what goes on upstairs?"

"Fellas, I can inform you now that all the officers and members of your Cat Club except Pickles, the Fire Cat, and Florio, who's in Florida, are parked in pleasant rooms on floors above."

"You bum!" exclaimed the tramps. "Why didn't you tell us sooner? You'd have saved us lots of worrying about old friends."

"I couldn't risk your running all over the Hotel to visit your pals," replied Tom.

"But Tom, it would be fun to say Hello to them," sighed Sinbad and The Duke.

"I suppose it would," admitted Tom. "Anyway, I've arranged for a little something. Listen."

Tom smoothed his white shirt front with a paw and, after summoning up his finest voice so that each elegant word would sound its best, he announced, *The President of the Cat Club cordially invites the members to a Stardust Ball, to be held in the Grand Ballroom of the Royal Hotel from midnight until dawn on the first night of the full moon. Brief business meeting to be followed with the sailor's hornpipe."*

Tom had expected the invitation to be welcomed with shouts of joy. But Sinbad and The Duke said quietly, "Is that all?"

"What more do you want?" groaned Tom. "I've arranged for your Club to meet in the grand ballroom of my Hotel. And you've been the first to receive an invitation. Our other guests don't get theirs until tomorrow night."

"But is that all?" persisted Sinbad and The Duke. "Isn't there any special message from those upstairs to us down here?"

"Yes. Checkers, who is helping me with social arrangements, wants you to carry an invitation in the morning to Pickles at the Fire House. Pickles needs to know early so that he can arrange to get the night off for the Ball."

130

"Why yes, of course," said they. "But we mean, isn't there a special message—just for us? Checkers is a great one for sending special little messages."

Then slowly something in the back of Tom's brain began to tick. "Ickety-wick . . ." A silly sounding word was coming back to him.

"Fellas," he said, "there's something I almost did forget. Checkers asked me to tell you, from him to you—"

"What?" they demanded.

"Ickety-wick-wick-wick," said Tom.

"Ickety-wick-wick-wick," echoed Sinbad and The Duke. And they grinned so happily that Tom became curious.

"What does that rubbish mean?" he asked.

"Oh," said they, "it's just a little something good old Checkers wanted us to know."

Sinbad and The Duke would say no more, and Tom himself thought no more about such nonsense. His mind was busy with the next steps toward the Stardust Ball.

On the following night, Tom delivered the invitations to the other guests, who received them joyfully and caused him no further trouble. And the humans were no problem. Mrs. Wilkins had obtained permission for the Club to use the ballroom. She also talked frequently, by telephone, with Captain Tinker, who was seeing to it that the cat owners would get the Club members to the ballroom on time.

It was Master Checkers who kept Tom on the go. Checkers had thrown his heart and soul into the social arrangements and was doing his very best to give brilliance to the

132

Stardust Ball. He paid special attention to the line of march and to the places the members would occupy in their procession as it entered the ballroom. Several times Checkers altered the places of the marchers, and each time—if Tom didn't mind—the new plan had to be okayed by the President and conveyed to the members.

The young Hotel Cat almost ran his legs off as he carried messages from floor to floor. He didn't mind. He enjoyed the satisfaction that comes with doing a good job. He loved the fun of being the manager of a truly grand affair.

The Line of March

On the evening of the first night of the full moon, there was great excitement in the cellar of the old Royal Hotel. Mr. Fred, the Furnace Man, whose knowledge of cat talk was limited, had received a personal invitation from Mrs. Wilkins to peek in on the Stardust Ball. Mr. Fred was now putting on his Sunday clothes. Tom, Sinbad, and The Duke were polishing their fur.

Shortly before midnight, the three cats climbed the cellar stairs. At the first floor,

they moved over to the grand stairway and slowly, with great dignity, began to mount the marble treads. The stairway, as usual, was deserted, though in its shadows still lingered the glamor of a bygone time.

135

"Scratch me. I must be dreaming," said Sinbad to The Duke.

The Duke reached out a paw and biffed Sinbad gently on the cheek.

At the second-floor landing, Tom turned left and guided his companions into the small, square room, or lobby, that served as entrance to the ballroom.

"Wait here," he said. "Your friends will soon be coming."

While Sinbad and The Duke seated themselves in the lobby, the young Hotel Cat walked to the ballroom door, which had been flung wide open. From the threshold he cast his eyes about the long lofty room to make sure that everything was as it should be.

Tom gasped at the loveliness of what he beheld. The old grand ballroom, which had been dark for many a year, had indeed been brought to life. Brightness glittered from the crystal chandeliers. Stardust sparkled on the ballroom floor. The grand piano stood in its far corner, ready for anyone who might care to use it. Otherwise, there was no furniture to trip the dancers. Last but not least, the red velvet curtains at the tall windows had been pulled together to block off the gaze of curious outsiders. Every possible arrangement had been completed for the pleasure of the Cat Club.

Tom remained standing just inside the doorway. Here he was to welcome the Club members as they marched into the ballroom. Here, as the Hotel Cat, proud of his work, he would enjoy his own Big Moment.

Ears and whiskers told him that the Big Moment was approaching. Cats were astir on all floors of the Hotel. Down here on the second floor, when he glanced through the lobby and along the hall, Tom saw his four friends, the cats of 811, emerging from the passage where his Lady, Mrs. Wilkins, lived. Edward, Checkers, Jenny, and Jack Tar were now advancing slowly, shoulder to shoulder, toward the ballroom, and Jenny

was wearing her bright red scarf. Behind them came little Mrs. Wilkins in her shiniest long skirt, and by her side walked tall Captain Tinker.

When the group reached the lobby, Mrs. Wilkins and the Captain quietly disappeared. Edward, Jenny, and Jack sat down with Sinbad and The Duke. Checkers, his black and white fur slicked down with spit, glided forward and gazed at the ballroom. "Tom!" he exclaimed. "It looks simply wonderful!" Then he stepped into a place beside the Hotel Cat.

Master Checkers had kept a paw on social arrangements. He had told the Hotel Cat, "Most of the Club members are only voices to you—voices from behind closed doors. You won't know half of the faces. You'll need someone to tell you who's who. And anyway, I'll have to name each name to you, because that's how it should be done."

So Checkers had appointed himself to stand with Tom while the Club members marched into the room. And now that the Big Moment was almost here, Tom found comfort in having the friendly young one at his side.

From the elevator midway down the hall, stepped a big yellow cat, wearing a fire helmet. "Good!" said Checkers. "Pickles, the Fire Cat, managed to get here. He came with Fireman Joe."

Cats of all sizes and colors began to fill the lobby and to chatter like old friends. The owners of these cats were probably not far behind, but they remained out of sight.

A hush fell over the lobby as a portly white cat slowly descended the grand stairway. He entered the lobby without saying a word and seated himself apart from the others. "Our President," whispered Checkers to Tom. "But someone is missing."

Suddenly, as if by unseen hands, a lively mass of silvery fur was plumped down on the lobby floor. "Madame Butterfly," murmured Checkers. "Now everyone is here."

The President rose, glanced sternly at his flock, and said, "Fall in line." There was a patter of paws, a rush this way and that way, as members sought their places for the line of march. Then the President picked his way forward and stood in front of Tom.

"Mr. President, may I present Tom of the Royal Hotel," said Checkers.

Tom bowed, and the President, in a gracious though solemn manner, said, "Tom, my personal thanks for all you have done for the Cat Club." And the portly President moved on toward the grand piano.

Next in the procession came another white cat, but she was a slim and slithery one. "Secretary Concertina—Tom of the Royal Hotel," said Checkers.

Tom bowed, and Concertina, with a smile, said, "Thank you, Tom, for bringing me news of this affair for my Club records."

And Concertina followed the trail of the President.

"Madame Butterfly from distant Persia—" announced Checkers.

Tom bowed, and Madame Butterfly, in a voice as silvery as her fur, said, "Tom, you saved my life that night when I got lost on the grand stairway. My heartfelt thanks." And the beauty sailed on.

"Solomon, the Club Inventor—"

Tom bowed, and Solomon, a wizened cat whose whiskers were dyed red, squeaked, "Tom, in a cupboard of my room I found the wire and screws I needed. My television set for cats will soon be working, thanks to your Hotel."

Next, marching side by side, came Honorary Member Jack Tar, Ship's Cat aboard the good ship *Sea Queen*, and Honorary Member Pickles, Fire Cat at Hook and Ladder Company 7X of the New York City Fire Department. Jack, whom Tom knew very well, smiled pleasantly, while Pickles, whom

Tom had never met, raised a merry paw to his fire helmet, saluted the Hotel Cat, and said, "Greetings from the whole Fire Department."

By now, the Big Whiskers of the Cat Club had passed, and the last half of the procession, which consisted of members who, because of their age or importance, were often called the Little Whiskers, moved more quickly.

The President's nephew Junior, Macaroni (the fancy dancer), Arabella and Antonio (the sweethearts), Romulus and Remus (the twins)—each gave a bow or a nod to the Hotel Cat and marched on. Then came Tom's young friends, Edward and Jenny, whose age had placed them near the tail end

143

of the procession. Both of them had a serious air but said Hi to Tom before they, in
their turn, marched away.

Lastly came Sinbad and The Duke, who
had been serving as the rear scouts. "Did
everyone get in all right?" they asked.

"Smooth as a whisker," replied Checkers.
And then he said to Tom, "See you later,"
and trotted over to the Club.

Tom's Big Moment, standing at the doorway and welcoming the members of the
Cat Club as they trooped into the ballroom,
had come and gone.

The Stardust Ball

Now that the procession had passed, it seemed to the young Hotel Cat that his Big Moment at the doorway had not lasted very long. He felt that the Cat Club had wasted no time in getting to the meeting. The last half of the procession had almost raced by him. His friends Edward and Jenny had only said Hi to him. Checkers had dashed off as soon as there were no more introductions to be made. Sinbad and The Duke remained with their Hotel Cat, but even they seemed eager to be on their way.

Tom glanced across the ballroom and saw the members gathering in a group that shone more brightly than anything in the ballroom. It was as if they'd brought their own glow with them. They really didn't need the crystal chandeliers, and they no longer seemed to need the Hotel Cat. Tom felt left out of everything.

"Come on, Tom, shake a leg," said Sinbad and The Duke.

"Fellas, I'm tired. I think I'll stay at the doorway. I can keep an eye on things from here."

"But, Tom, you'll hear what 'Ickety-wick-wick-wick' is all about. And anyway, you promised to attend the business meeting."

"Why, so I did," he stammered.

Thus Tom let Sinbad and The Duke take him to the meeting ground, which was at the grand piano. On a front ledge of the piano, with a front paw dangling above the keys, lay Secretary Concertina. The rest of the Club had formed a circle on the floor.

At the head of the circle, near the foremost leg of the piano, sat the President. On his right sat Madame Butterfly, and on his left, the two honorary members, the Ship's Cat and the Fire Cat. Other members had seated themselves so that altogether the Club formed a bright, warm, furry ring—a family circle to which Tom did not belong.

Somewhere in the circle was an empty space just big enough for three cats.

"Reserved seats," laughed Sinbad and The Duke. "Tom, squeeze in and sit between us."

And that is how Tom found himself sitting with the Cat Club. He sat rather stiffly, so as to make it clear he was there on Hotel business—nothing more.

"The meeting will come to order," announced the President.

Concertina, from her perch on the piano,

stretched down her right front paw, hit the keys, and *zing!* the President's words were put on record.

"Our business meeting," continued the President, "shall open with a poem written especially for the occasion by our Songster Edward. The Songster has the floor."

Edward, who had been sitting with Checkers and Jenny, rose. He looked handsome in his tiger stripes, but rather young to be the Songster of the Cat Club. Tom hoped, for Edward's sake, that the poem, whatever it was, would not be a flop.

"Mr. President," said Edward in a round voice that showed no trace of nervousness, "my poem is an ode—a poem in praise of." Then Edward, after glancing around the circle to make sure he had the attention of everyone, including Tom, continued, "It's called 'Poem in Praise of Our Hotel Cat.' "

Tom could scarcely believe his ears. But Concertina zingged the title into the records, and Edward began:

149

POEM IN PRAISE OF OUR HOTEL CAT

When boilers burst and we had to leave home,
No need to roam.
The Royal Hotel offered room and bed,
And Tom, the Hotel Cat, graciously said,
"A cat who comes here
Will find good cheer
And a home—a home away from home—
Beneath this dome."

The Cat Club arrived and settled in,
And now the Club would like to begin
A song in praise of Tom the Cat,
Who sees to this and sees to that.
For Tom's a cat with an open mind
And a heart as brave as it is kind.
Tom answers calls,
Patrols the halls,
Arranges for balls
Within the walls
Of his Hotel—the Royal Hotel—
With its musty smells that somehow tell
Of the elegant ways
Of olden days.
But the hour that's here is not to be sneezed at—
Not by a cat, oh, not by a cat
On a glorious night
When the moon shines bright
And Tom has opened the ballroom door
And stardust covers the ballroom floor.

The Songster's voice died away, and the President said, "Thank you, Edward."

But the beautiful words of the poem lingered in the air, wrapped themselves around Tom, and drew him closer to the warmth and brightness of the Cat Club. He glanced at the members to find out, if he could, what they thought about the poem. A few paws were twitching in the stardust, as if eager to begin the hornpipe. Yet no one really moved. It was as if the hour for dancing had not come.

Indeed, the President was saying, "The purpose of this meeting is to discuss special business that has arisen since our Club moved into the Royal. Jenny, who was among the first to arrive, knows as well as anyone what may require our attention. I have asked Jenny to bring Club business up-to-date. Jenny has the floor."

The little black cat rose, lifted her chin out of her red scarf, and looked straight at the President.

"Mr. President," she said in her shy but steadiest voice, "our business is about a cat known in the secret code of our Club by the name of Ickety-wick-wick-wick. His real name is Tom. I move that Tom, the Hotel Cat of the Royal, be elected an honorary member of the Cat Club."

"We second the motion," cried Sinbad and The Duke.

The President said, "All those in favor of Tom's election will kindly raise a right front paw."

Every right front paw shot upward.

Specks of stardust were drifting back to the floor as the President declared, "I am pleased to announce that Tom, the Royal Hotel Cat—and a great Hotel Cat—is now, like the Ship's Cat and the Fire Cat, an honorary member of the Cat Club. May Tom come to our meetings whenever he can."

Zing! went the piano.

"Friends forever," sang the Cat Club.

"Me," thought Tom to himself, "me, me!"

Sinbad and The Duke nudged him and whispered, "Say something."

Tom rose and said, "Mr. President and you, my friends, I thank you for electing me an honorary member of your joyful band."

When Tom sat down, he realized he should have said something more.

The President was saying, "If there is no further business . . ."

Tom raised a paw.

"Tom has the floor," said the President.

"Mr. President," began Tom, "it's about the arrangements for the Stardust Ball. Those of us who hold jobs among the humans know that in big undertakings, like this Ball, there are often a few people who lend a hand."

"Hear, hear!" cried the Ship's Cat.

"Hear, hear!" echoed the Fire Cat.

And the Hotel Cat went on to say, "Two people in particular have helped to make our Ball possible. They are Mrs. Wilkins, who has long been a guest at the Royal, and Captain Tinker, whom you all know."

Zing! Zing! And those two names went into the records with an extra flourish.

But Tom had not finished. He said, "Mrs. Wilkins and Captain Tinker are now sitting out there in the lobby, beyond our view, on gold chairs that once belonged to the ballroom. I suggest that Mrs. Wilkins and the Captain would do us great honor if they came to the doorway and received our thanks."

The President nodded, and the members, with a thrill of excitement, lined up in a row with him and faced the doorway. Tom disappeared into the lobby and brought Mrs. Wilkins and the Captain to the threshold. He stayed behind them while the Club burst into shouts of "Thank you, Mrs. Wilkins! Thank you, Captain Tinker! Paws and claws forever at your service—day and night."

Little Mrs. Wilkins waved a hand; the tall graceful Captain bowed. Tom then led the couple back to the gold chairs and returned to his Club.

"Tom, is that all?" asked the President.

"Yes, Mr. President," Tom answered quickly, for his happiness was such that he could scarcely keep his four paws on the floor.

"Our business meeting is over," declared the President.

Concertina gave a final thump on the piano and hustled down to join the others.

"The hour has come for us to dance," announced the President. "Let us not forget we are in the ballroom of the Royal. Let us dance on velvet paws. And now, choose partners."

Mr. President offered a paw to Madame Butterfly. Tom, of course, chose little Jenny. Concertina nabbed Checkers. And so it went, until every cat had a partner.

"One, two, three, rise!" called the President.

Up rose Tom on his hind legs, and with a kick at the stardust, he and all the other cats began the sailor's hornpipe. Skip, skip, skip

and leap. And oh, the joy of sailing through
the air with Jenny at his side!

Tom danced the second round with Madame Butterfly, and the third with Concertina. But he did not neglect the Little Whiskers. In fact, as the night wore on, he did a
turn with everyone, while the hornpipe
cry—Heigh-ho, heigh-ho!—rang out sweetly
through the ballroom.

158

Then, in the wee small morning hours, a Little Whisker somewhere in the crowd slipped and bumped his bottom. He rose quickly and laughed to show he was not hurt. But other Little Whiskers stopped their dancing and began to giggle and talk sleepy nonsense.

Mr. President lost no time. He jumped onto the piano and called, "Attention, please."

Dancers dropped to their four paws, and everyone faced the President.

"Dawn is here. The hour has come to end the Stardust Ball," he said.

"Ice cream!" cried a shrill young voice.

Mr. President cast a withering glance at his nephew, and after that he said to one and all, "Those of you who leave in good order will find refreshments waiting for you in your rooms. Tom, Sinbad, and The Duke shall leave first. They know what to do and where to go."

After the Ball
Was Over

Tom left the ballroom with Sinbad and The Duke and went straight to his Lady, Mrs. Wilkins. She and Captain Tinker were still sitting on their gold chairs in the lobby.

"My Lady, the Stardust Ball is over," said Tom.

"So soon?" she murmured in a wondering voice. But she rose and bade good night to Captain Tinker and let the three cats escort her slowly and in silence down the hall to the door of her room.

There Tom broke the silence. "Did you have fun?" he asked her.

"This has been a night to remember," replied Mrs. Wilkins. And she added, "How proud I am of the young Hotel Cat who has become the newest member of the Cat Club."

"And a friend forever!" cried Sinbad and The Duke.

Mrs. Wilkins fumbled for her key, entered her room, and closed the door.

"Don't forget to lock your door," called Tom.

Tom of the Royal waited until he heard the key turn in its lock. Then he scampered upstairs with Sinbad and The Duke to enjoy an after-the-ball snack with the cats in 811. For among the members of the Cat Club— all friends forever—nothing ever really ends.

ESTHER AVERILL (1902–1992) began her career as a storyteller drawing cartoons for her local newspaper. After graduating from Vassar College in 1923, she moved first to New York City and then to Paris, where she founded her own publishing company. The Domino Press introduced American readers to artists from all over the world, including Feodor Rojankovsky, who later won a Caldecott Award.

In 1941, Averill returned to the United States and found a job in the New York Public Library while continuing her work as a publisher. She wrote her first book about the red-scarfed, mild-mannered cat Jenny Linsky in 1944, modeling its heroine on her own shy cat. Averill would eventually write twelve more tales about Miss Linsky and her friends (including the I Can Read Book *The Fire Cat*), each of which was eagerly awaited by children all over the United States (and their parents, too).